the BAD GUYS

EPISODE

7

DO-YOU-THINK-HE-SAURUS?!

A SCHOLASTIC PRESS BOOK
FROM SCHOLASTIC AUSTRALIA

SCHOLASTIC PRESS
345 PACIFIC HIGHWAY LINDFIELD NSW 2070
AN IMPRINT OF SCHOLASTIC AUSTRALIA PTY LIMITED
(ABN 11 000 614 577)
PO BOX 579 GOSFORD NSW 2250
WWW.SCHOLASTIC.COM.AU

PART OF THE SCHOLASTIC GROUP
SYDNEY • AUCKLAND • NEW YORK • TORONTO • LONDON • MEXICO CITY
• NEW DELHI • HONG KONG • BUENOS AIRES • PUERTO RICO

FIRST PUBLISHED BY SCHOLASTIC AUSTRALIA IN 2018.

NATIONAL LIBRARY OF AUSTRALIA

A CATALOGUE RECORD FOR THIS BOOK IS AVAILABLE FROM THE NATIONAL LIBRARY OF AUSTRALIA

ISBN: 978-93-5275-541-7 (PAPERBACK)

TYPESET IN JANSON, ELO, KERBEROS FANG AND BEHANCE.
DESIGN BY NICOLE STOFBERG AND SARAH MITCHELL.

FIRST EDITION : 2018
THIS EDITION : OCTOBER 2021
PRINTED IN INDIA

AARON BLABEY

the BAD GUYS

EPISODE 7

DO-YOU-THINK-HE-SAURUS?!

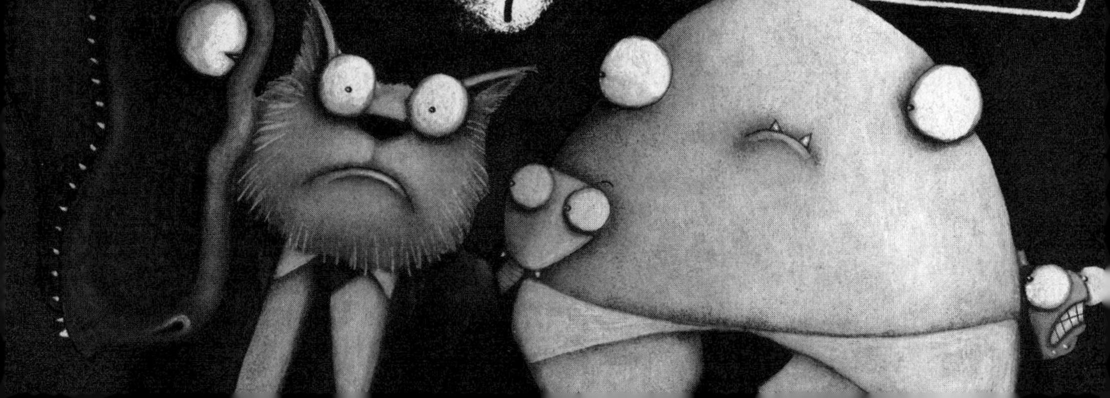

GG

Dave?
Tell me you're filming this?
6 NEWS
6
CREW
DAVE
CAMERA OPERATOR
6

Film it yourself, Fluffit! I'm out of here . . .
Come back, you coward! The **GOOD GUYS CLUB** will save us!
TY
XIT

ZOOOOM!

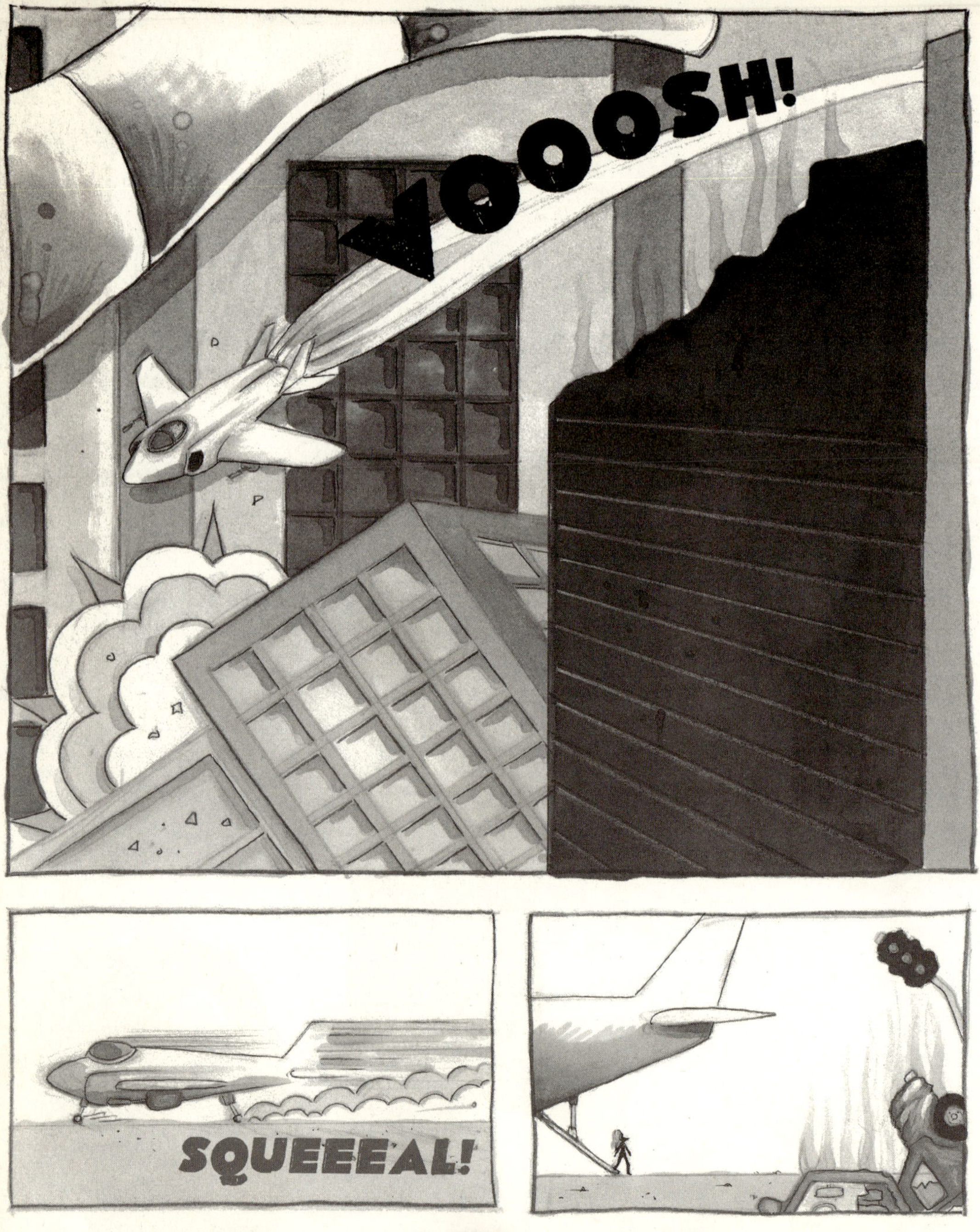
VOOOSH!
SQUEEEAL!

Hey lady!
You KNOW we don't
have time for this.
Just give me a minute . . .

THIS was the arranged
LANDING POINT.
THIS is where Mr Wolf and the boys were meant to return to Earth.

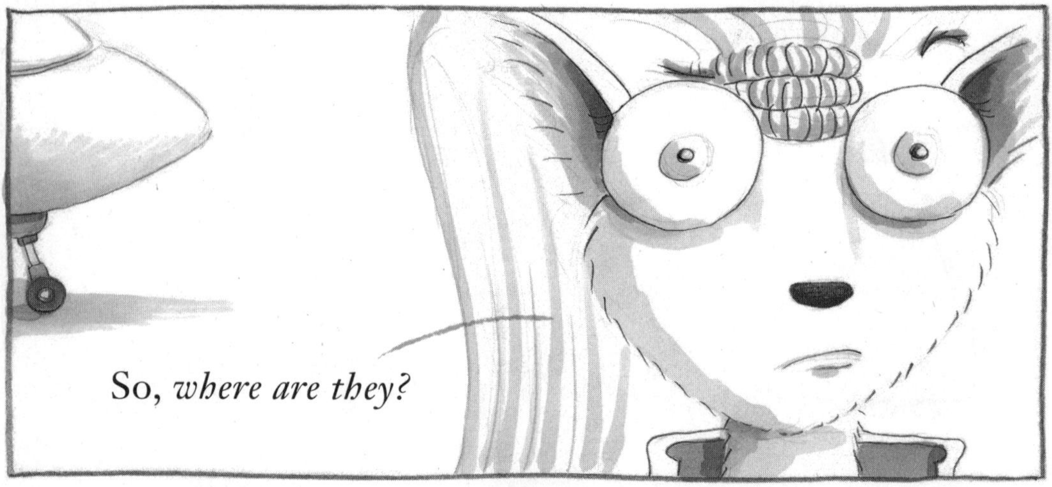
So, *where are they?*

FREEZE!

FOX!
GET OUT
OF THERE!
Stay calm, guys.
Everything will be cool . . .

YOU HAVE BEEN IDENTIFIED
AS AN ENEMY.
PREPARE TO BE
TERMINATED.
Uh-oh . . .

On second thoughts, team . . .
I'd like to ask a favour . . .
Take care of the
BAD GUYS
for me?
ZAP!

FOX?!

· CHAPTER 1 ·

RIGHT PLACE, WRONG TIME

65 MILLION YEARS EARLIER . . .

We were on our way to

SAVE EARTH

from an **ALIEN INVASION**

but our Escape Pod turned out to be a

TIME MACHINE

so *instead*, we've ended up in

the distant past surrounded by

DINOSAURS.

Have I got

that *right?!*

Ahhh . . . yep.
That sounds about right.

Well then—*nobody move!*
If there's one thing I know
about dinosaurs, it's this—
if you **DON'T MOVE**
they **CAN'T SEE YOU** . . .

WINK!

Wolf, they can TOTALLY see you . . .

You'd *think* that, wouldn't you?
But, NO! I'm *completely invisible*.
Isn't it amazing?

Wolfie!
You're thinking of the
TYRANNOSAURUS REX.
These are **VELOCIRAPTORS.**
And they can TOTALLY
see you . . .

Oh, I don't think so . . .

Chico, they're looking into your *soul.*
And it looks tasty.
You look like *soul food*, bro.

Hmm, I know it
looks that way . . .
But I'm *pretty* confident
if I just keep really still
I'll be perfectly—
SNAP!

OH MY STARS! I THINK THEY CAN SEE ME!
FLING!
Yep. He's got it now.

Well, amigos . . .
in Bolivia we have an old saying—

*It's better to be eaten by dinosaurs
than it is to be eaten by aliens
with butts for hands.*

Don't feel sad yet, soldier . . .

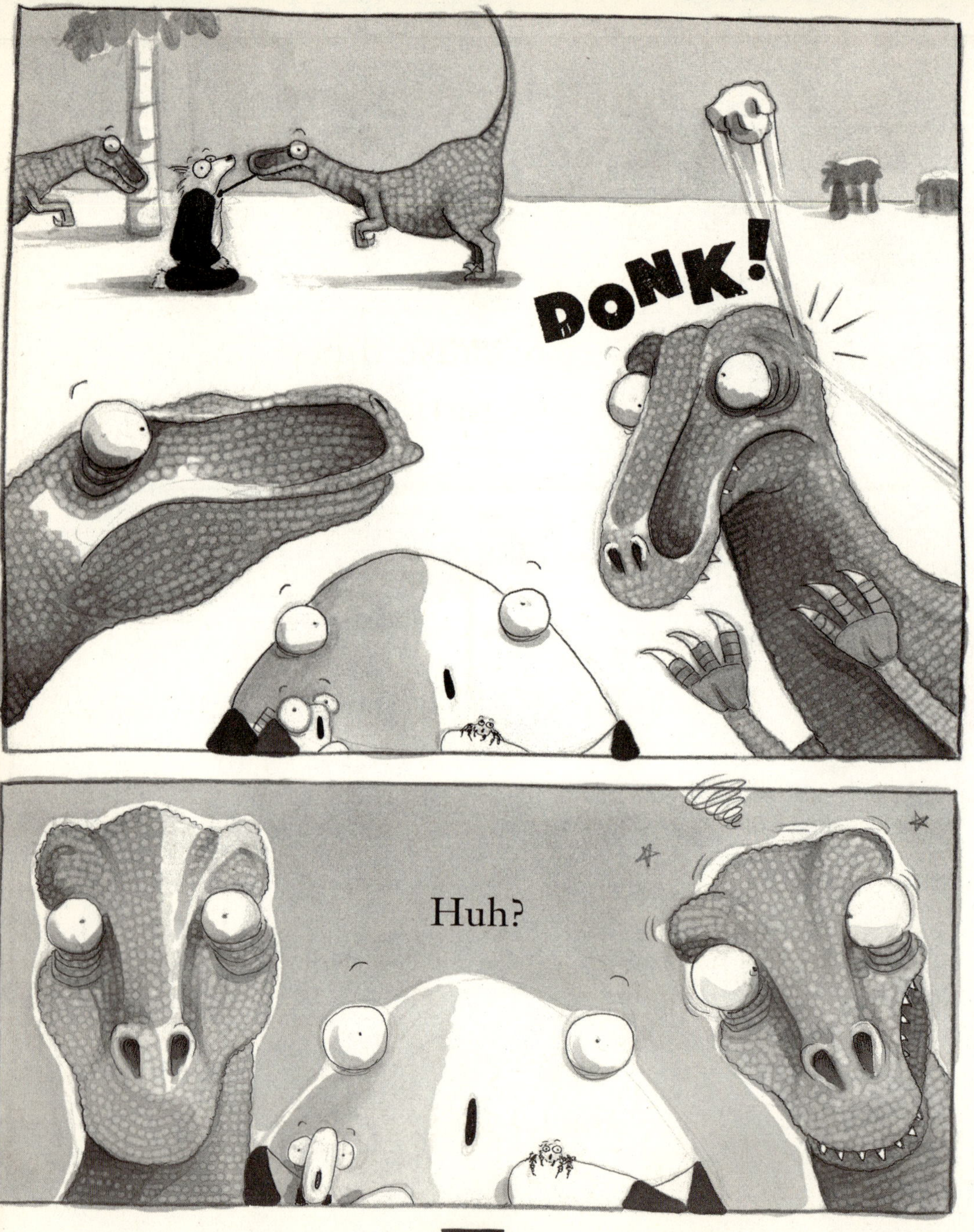
DONK!
Huh?

. . . because this party
is just getting started!

Now, who wants a piece of me?
Snake?!
Wait a second, little buddy . . .
I've got this.
No, wait! We can take them on TOGETHER!

Will you two nutjobs stop trying to out-hero each other?
WHAT ARE WE GOING TO DO?!
Let's BOOGIE!
FLING!
SMACK!

Yeah, that's right!
COME AND GET IT.
MR PIRANHA?
MR TARANTULA?
We'll LEAD THEM AWAY!
You two need to fix the TIME MACHINE.
EEEE!
AARGGH!

MR WOLF?
MR SHARK?
AARRRGGGHH!
EEEEEEE!

You two need to stop screaming and **FOLLOW ME . . .**

Oh sure!
We'll just
'FIX THE
TIME MACHINE'.
ARE YOU
CRAZY?!
Oh chico!
Don't get me
wrong—
if anyone
can fix it,
YOU can . . .

No, no . . .
it's not that . . .
Then what?
Snake called me
'Mr Tarantula'!
I just feel really
PROUD . . .

• CHAPTER 2 •

GONE ROGUE

FOOMP!
Shhhhhhh . . .
Don't. Make.
A. Sound.
This way.
Stay close . . .
TUMBLE!
TUMBLE!
VOOSH!

Does he seem . . . different to you?
Well, saving us from Marmalade probably gave him a little confidence boost . . .
No . . . it's more than that. It's like he's . . . become the LEADER. Don't you think?
Well now, I wouldn't go THAT far . . .

FOOMP!
FREEZE!
That was close.
Now, keep low and
follow me . . .

Snake?!
Where are we going?
We have to get back to the
Time-Machine-thingy and get it working!
WE are the only ones who know
what's coming—the world is about to be
DESTROYED
BY ALIENS but we are
65 MILLION YEARS
away from the action!
WHAT ARE WE GOING
TO DO?!

THIS is what we're going to do—
we're going to DEAL WITH IT.
WOLF-UP, soldier! Right now!
We're going to save the world.
Say it!
We're going to
save the world . . .
And **THIS** is how
it's going to go down . . .

Mr Shark!
YOU are going to do
what you do best . . .
I see . . .
And what *kind* of disguise
would you like?
A tree.

Done.

Man, you are good at disguises . . .
Tell me something I don't know.
Wolf!
Climb the tree!

Now,
freeze!

Good.
Now, Tree?
Move silently through the jungle and get us to
HIGH GROUND.
I need to see the lay of the land.
Yes, sir!

Who *are* you?! And what have you done with Mr Snake?

• CHAPTER 3 •

SO MANY PROBLEMS

If this thing
zapped us millions of years
into the past by flying
SUPER-CRAZY-FAST,
how can it send us BACK if it's broken?

Hmmm, well that's the thing—
it got us BACK TO EARTH
by moving us quickly,
so yes, it definitely used
SPEED
to move us through SPACE . . .

But what I want to do is find the part of this contraption that moved us through
TIME.
That's a TOTALLY different thing. Don't you think?

Could you repeat the question?
Look— this little space pod blasted us down to Earth from the moon and put us exactly WHERE we need to be. We're in exactly the right PLACE.
BUT!

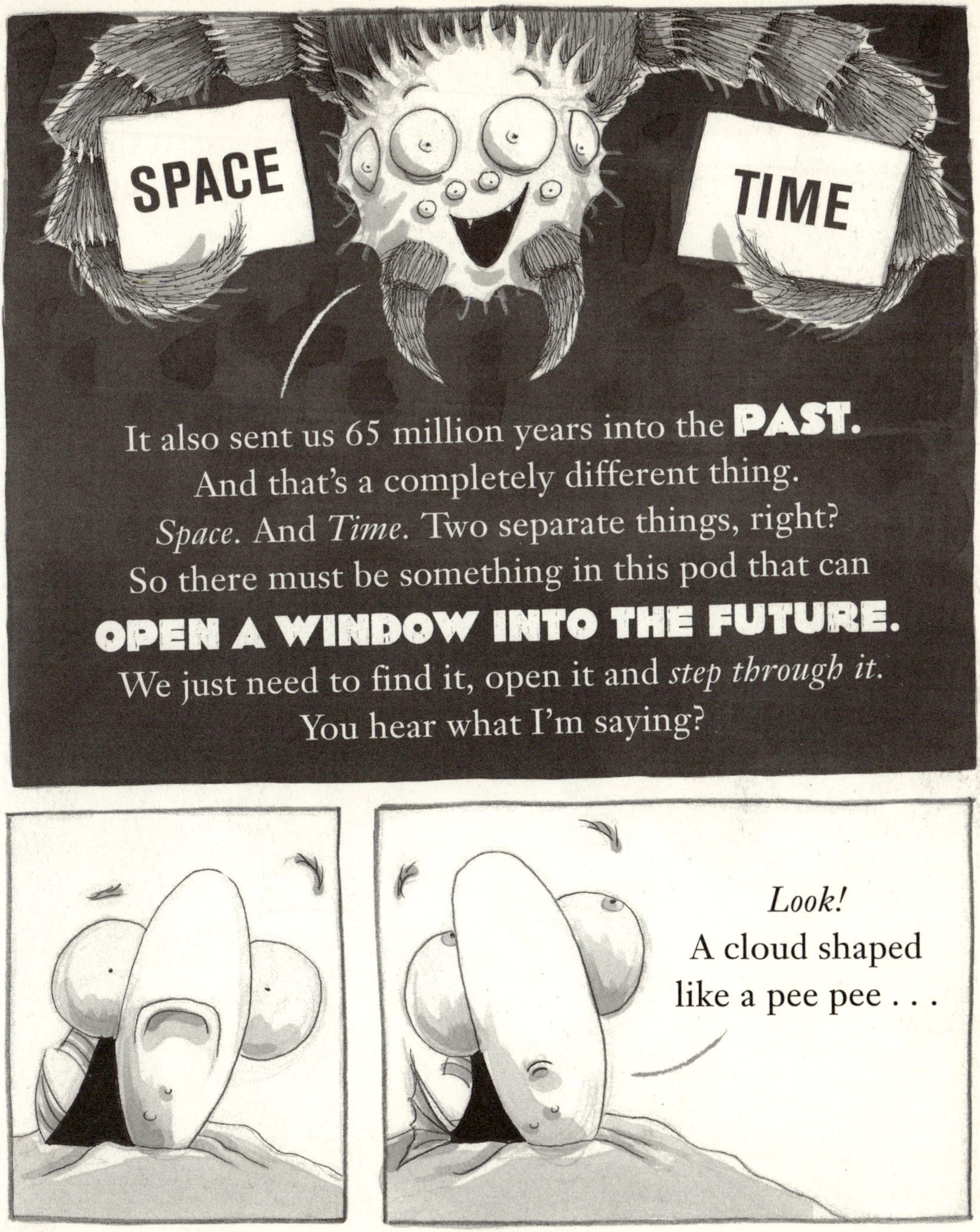
SPACE
TIME
It also sent us 65 million years into the **PAST.**
And that's a completely different thing.
Space. And *Time.* Two separate things, right?
So there must be something in this pod that can
OPEN A WINDOW INTO THE FUTURE.
We just need to find it, open it and *step through it.*
You hear what I'm saying?
Look!
A cloud shaped
like a pee pee . . .

So, all we need to do is identify the
TIME-TRAVEL DRIVE . . .
and if I had to guess . . .
I'd probably try to
hot-wire this bit and . . .
BOOM!

WHIZZ!

FLOP!
THUNK!
THUNK!
THUNK!

Well, *that* looks promising!

!
Could this be . . .
a *doorway to the future?*

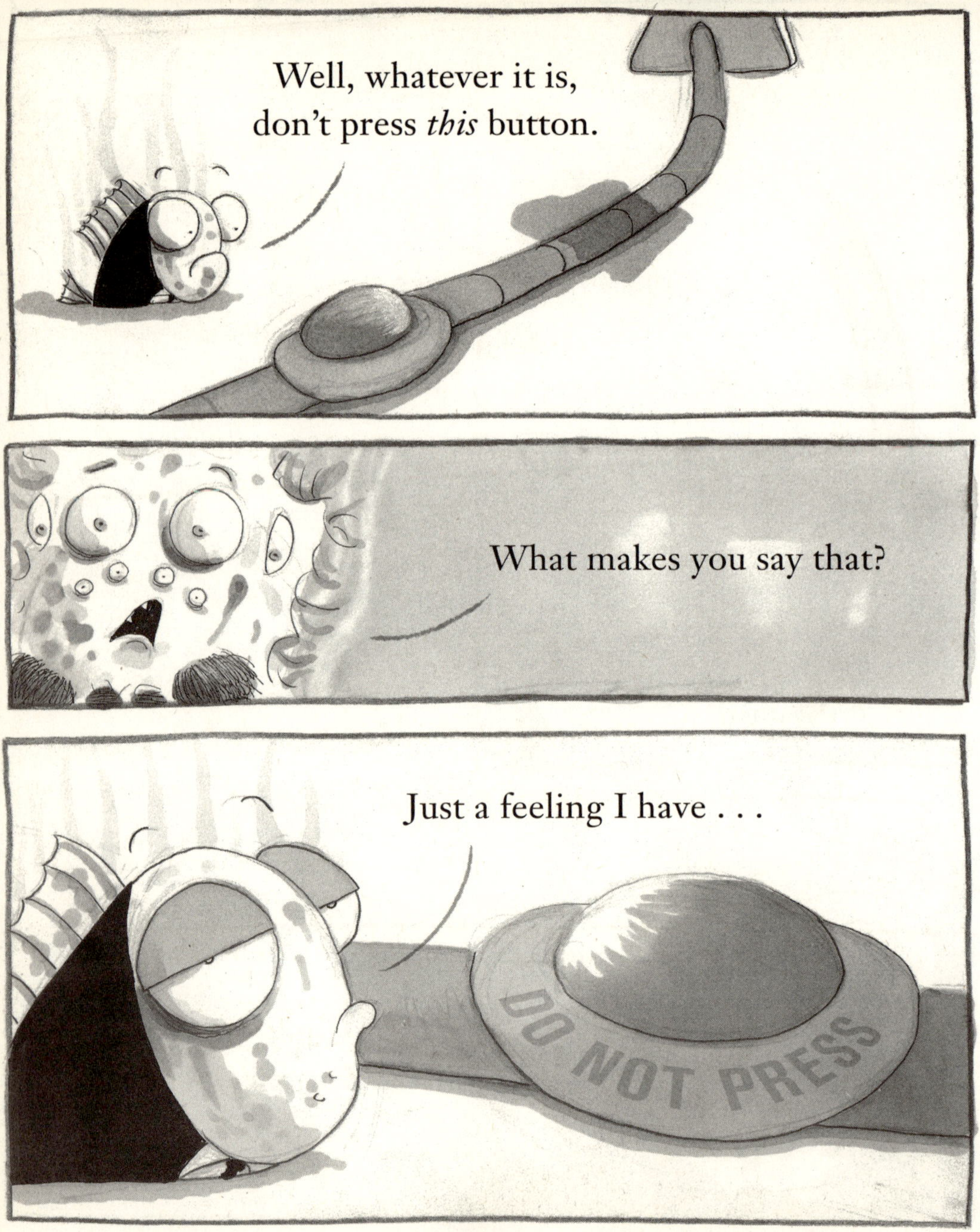
Well, whatever it is,
don't press *this* button.
What makes you say that?
Just a feeling I have . . .
DO NOT PRESS

That RING . . .
Don't you think it looks like a portal?
Like a *portal through time*, perhaps?

I'll just nod my head and
hopefully you'll be struck by
lightning before you can ask me
any more stupid questions . . .

But if it is . . .
a . . .
por . . . tal . . .
Then what?
Look, I didn't really want you to get struck by lightning, OK?

Mr . . .
Piranha . . .
Whatever you do—
DON'T.
MOVE.

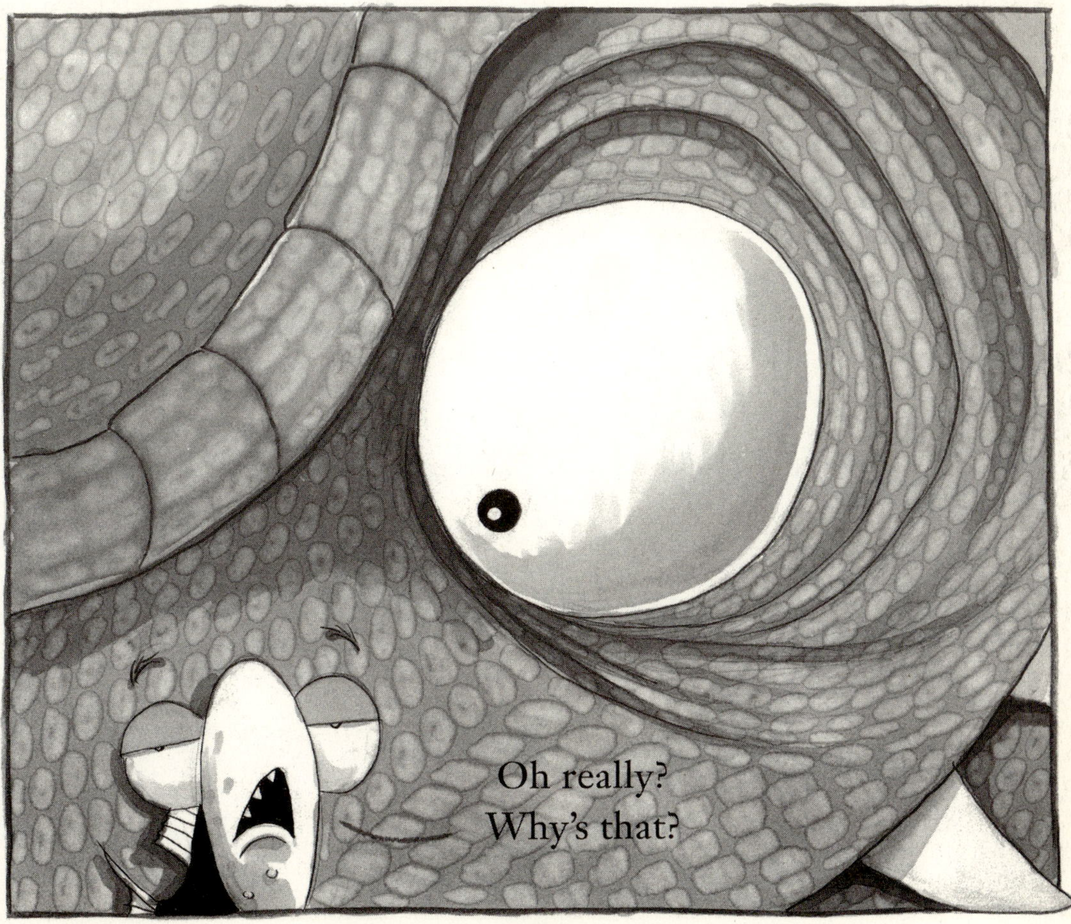
Oh really?
Why's that?

Wait—there isn't something behind me, is there?

It's a *Tyrannosaurus rex.* Their vision IS based on movement, so if you stay completely still—
ZOOOOM!
AAARRRRGGGHHHH!!!

R

OOOA-
ARR!
¡Ay caramba!

OK, stay cool, amigo . . .
Here's what you're going to do . . .

You're going to
move around a great deal.
THAT'S the key to success
in this situation . . .

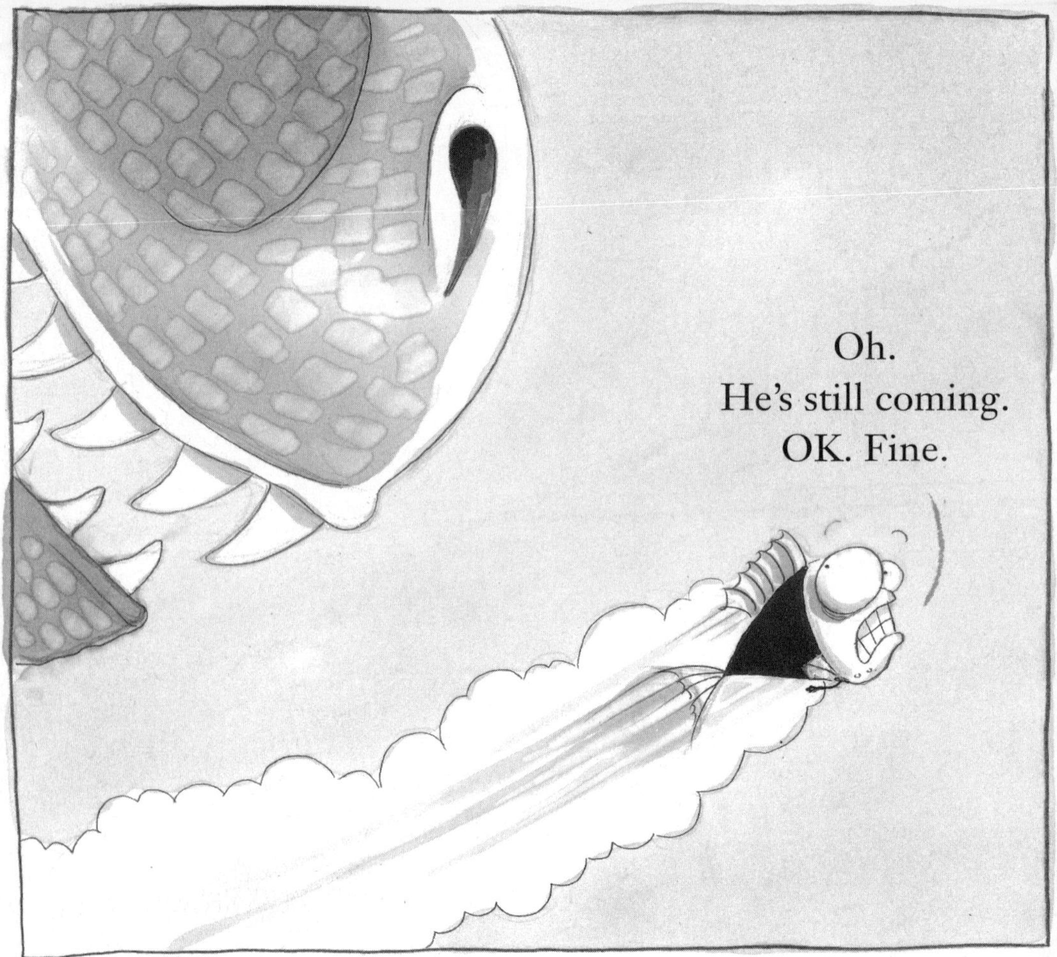
Oh.
He's still coming.
OK. Fine.

I've still got some moves.
How do you like . . .

THIS?!
BOING!
BOING!
BOING!
BOING!
BOING!

R

OOAR!

OK.
I'm in the deep poop.
AAEEEEEIIII!!

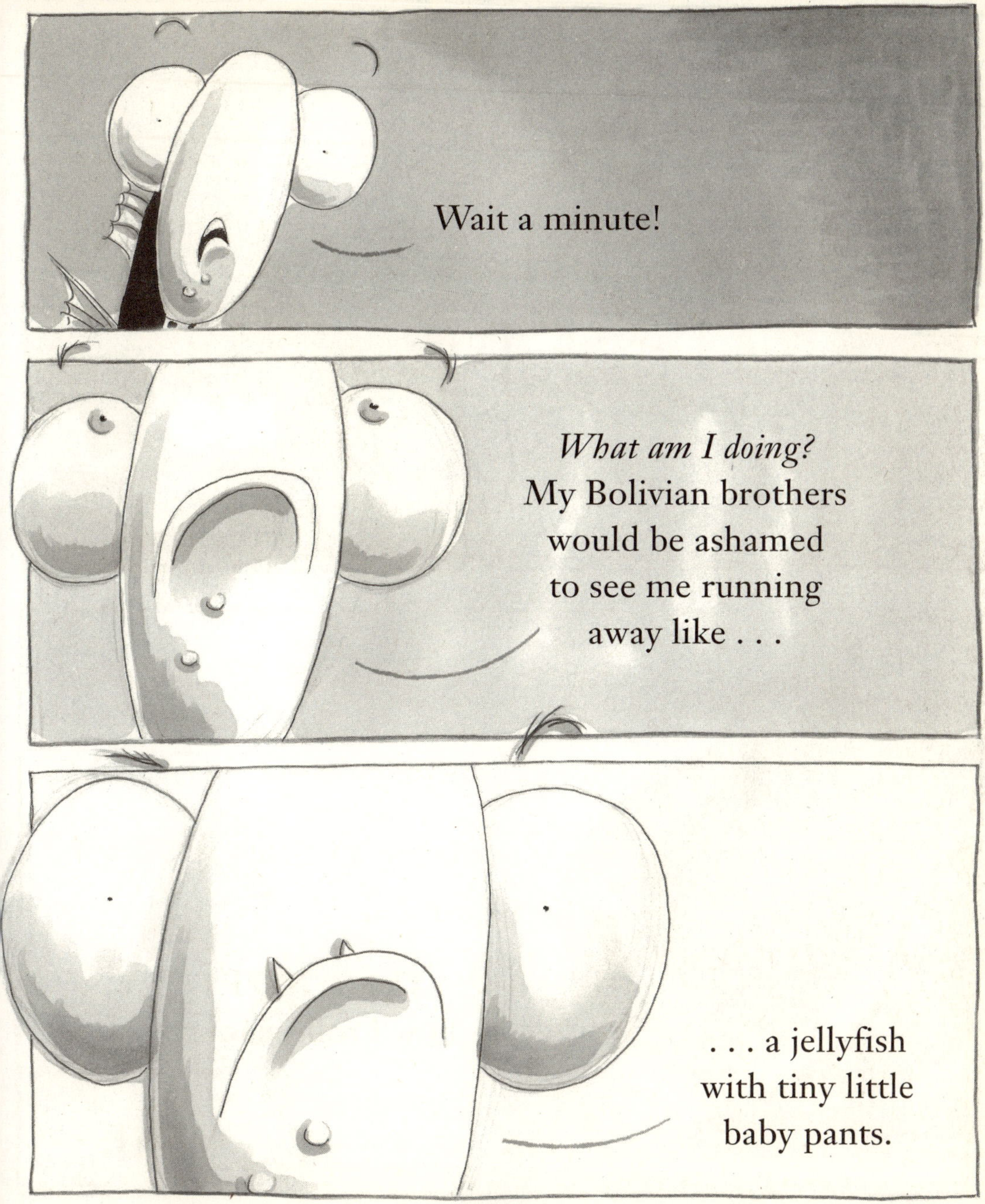
Wait a minute!
What am I doing?
My Bolivian brothers
would be ashamed
to see me running
away like . . .
. . . a jellyfish
with tiny little
baby pants.

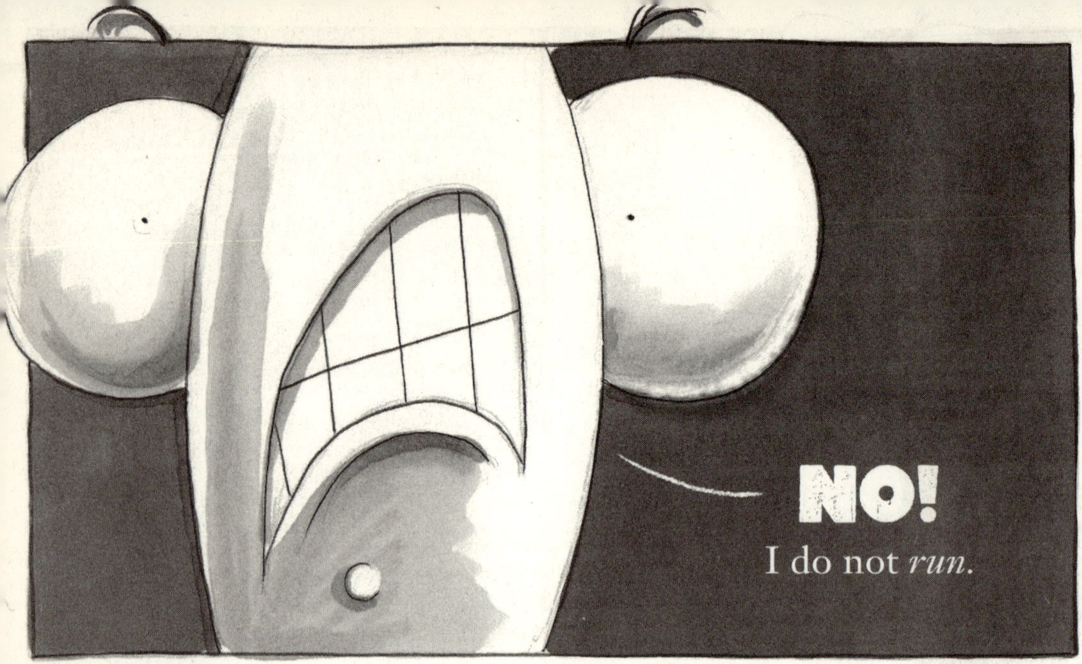
NO!
I do not *run*.

That is NOT
how I roll, señor.

I bring the THUNDER!
I bring the LIGHTNING!
I AM THE
PERFECT STORM!

TASTE THE FURY!
No, wait . . .
he's WAY too big . . .
SWIVEL!
SPLODGE!

No-one must
ever know
of this . . .

• CHAPTER 4 •

WHO'S RUNNING THIS SHOW?

Shhh, keep it down!
Legs is playing around
with some kind of contraption.
Where'd he get that from?
I don't see Piranha
anywhere . . .

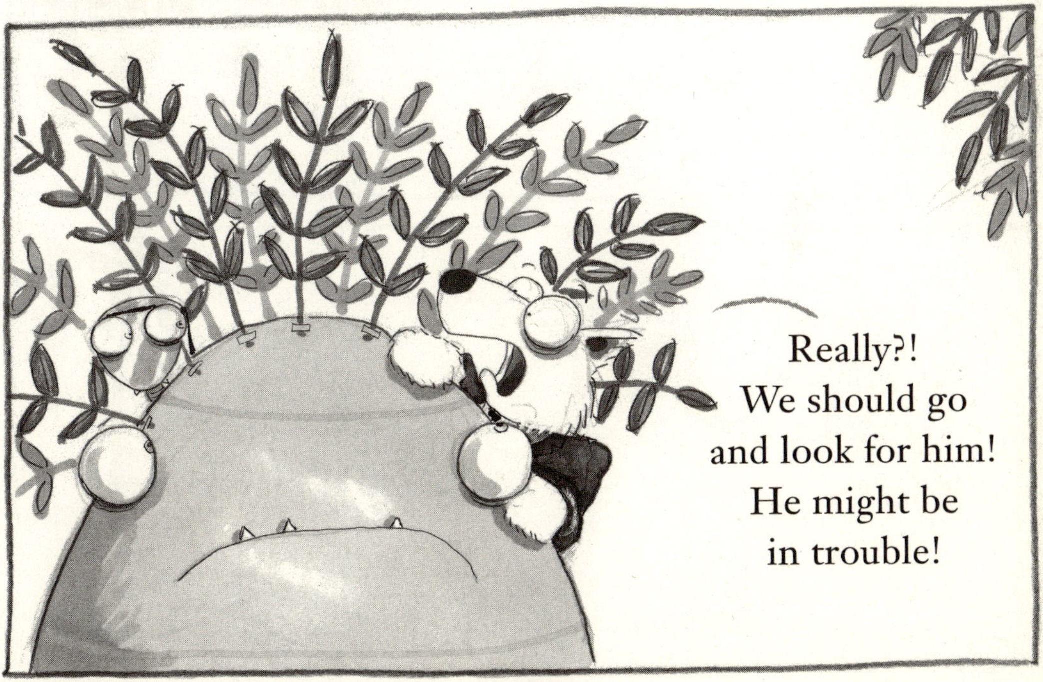
Really?!
We should go
and look for him!
He might be
in trouble!

Wolf! Listen to me—
WE are in trouble.
We are surrounded by
hungry Velociraptors
and all we have
to protect us is a
NAKED
SHARK
with some
BUSHES ON
HIS HEAD.

No offence,
big fella.
None taken.

Oh, man.
You're right
We *are* in trouble.
It's all right though.
We'll get out of this,
I promise.
But I need you
to stay *calm*.
Listen to him, Wolfie.
He knows what he's
talking about.

You're right, Mr Shark.
And you were right before—
it's almost like . . . our little team . . .
has a new . . . *leader.*
Isn't it? Hehehe.
Yeah.

Are you kidding?!
I don't want *your* job,
you hair-brained lunatic.
Who needs THAT
kind of responsibility?
I'm just your
wing-man.

Your
vastly superior
wing-man.

I really am so proud of you.
Yeah, yeah.
Whatever, man.

EEEEEEE!

That was *too* close.
I sure hope Mr Tarantula knows what he's doing.

• CHAPTER 5 •

THE PORTAL

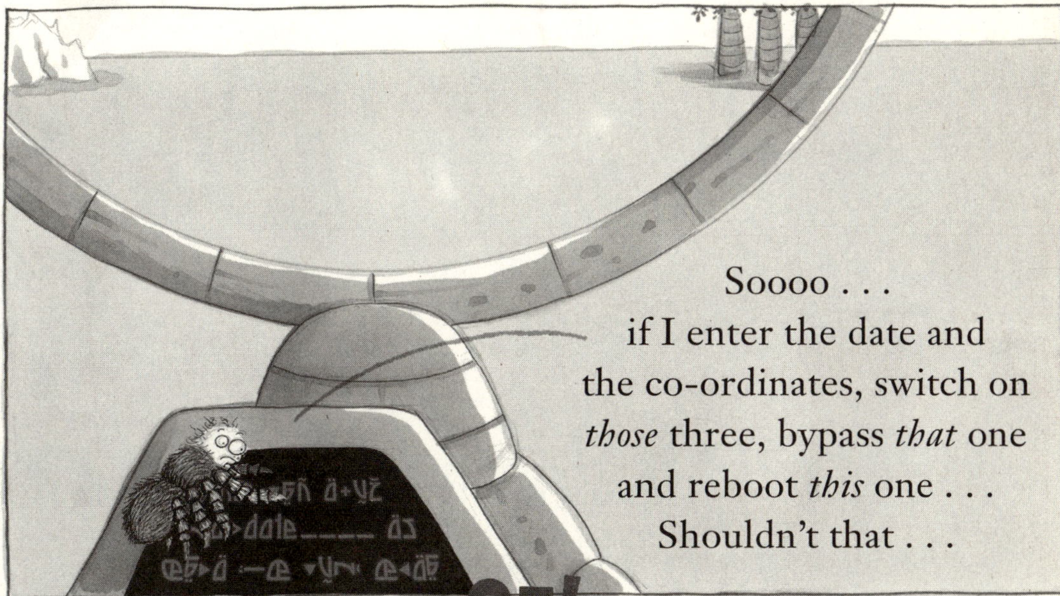

A VORTEX INTO ANOTHER DIMENSION!

Yeah. Pretty sure that's what it is.

Yep . . .

LOOK!

HE DID IT!
HE DID IT!
HE DID IT!

SHHHH!
You'll give us away!
Oh my stars, I'm SO sorry.
Tree!
Move *slowly* and *silently* away from this cliff-top, back through the jungle and down to the Time-Machine . . .
I'd love to . . .

But Mr Wolf
just rang the
DINNER BELL!

RUN!
No, Wolf! Wait a minute!
Aw, man,
I'm not wearing
any pants . . . .

SQUARK!
SQUARK!
AAAIIEEEE!!!

VOOOSH!
Oh no . . .
GRAB!
GRAB!

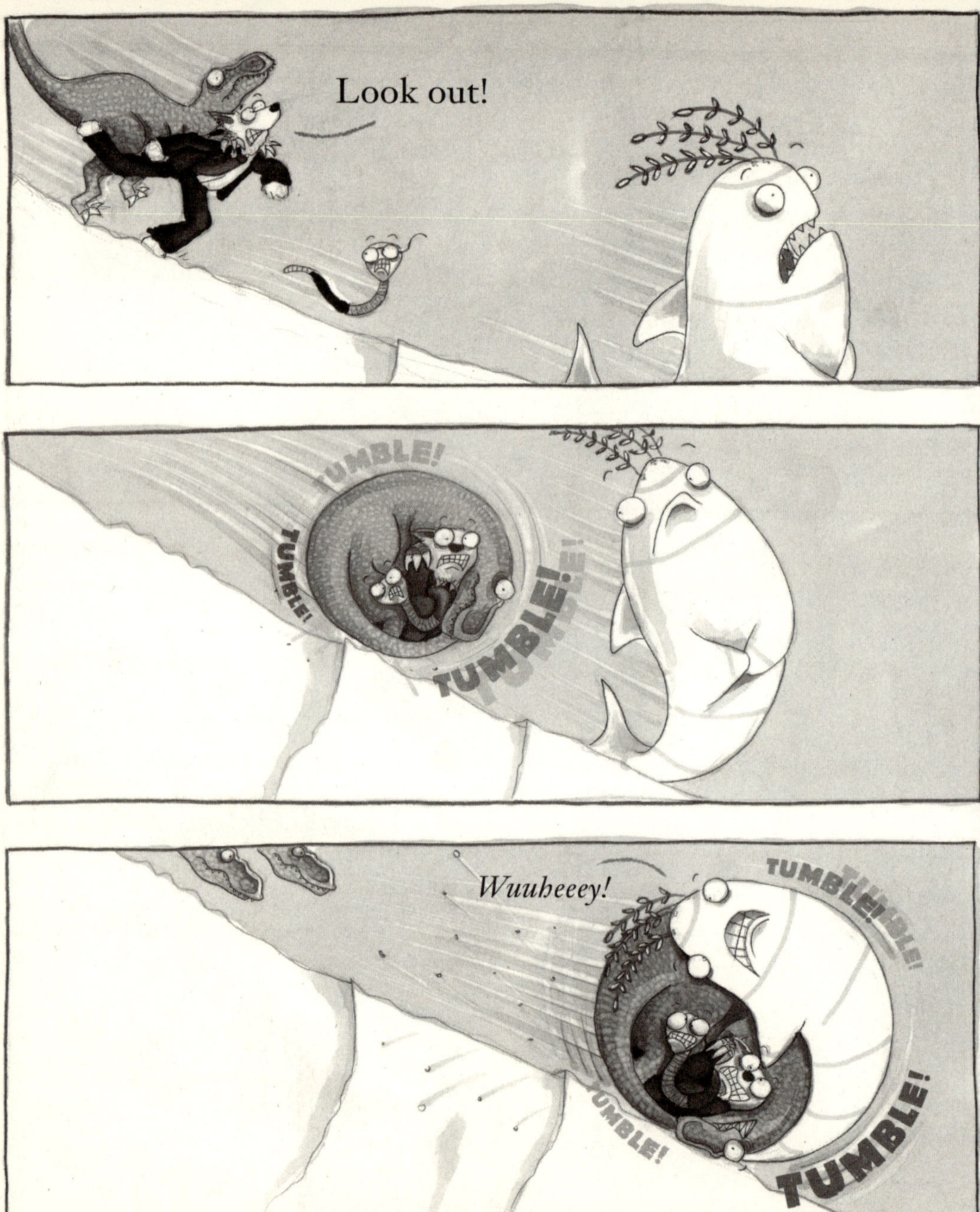
Look out!
TUMBLE!
TUMBLE!
TUMBLE!
TUMBLE!
TUMBLE!
Wuuheeey!
TUMBLE!
TUMBLE!
TUMBLE!
TUMBLE!

AAAAARRRGGGRGHHH!!
TUMBLE!
TUMBLE!
TUMBLE!

I'VE HAD ENOUGH OF THIS!
LET ME OUT OF THIS NOSTRIL!
PIRANHA! *Is that you?!*
No! No! It's not me! This is just a *dream*, chico! *I am not stuck in a dinosaur's nostril.*
You **NEVER SAW THIS,** understand?

WHOOOOSH!
SMACK!
YOU NEVER SAW THIS!

SPLURT!
DONK!
AAAIIEEEE!

Piranha!
It IS you!

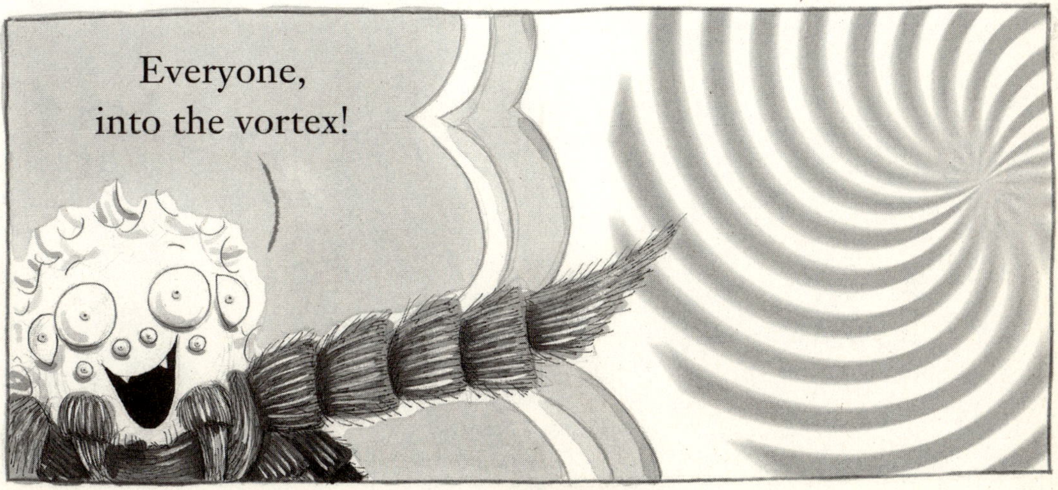
Everyone,
into the vortex!

FOLLOW
ME!

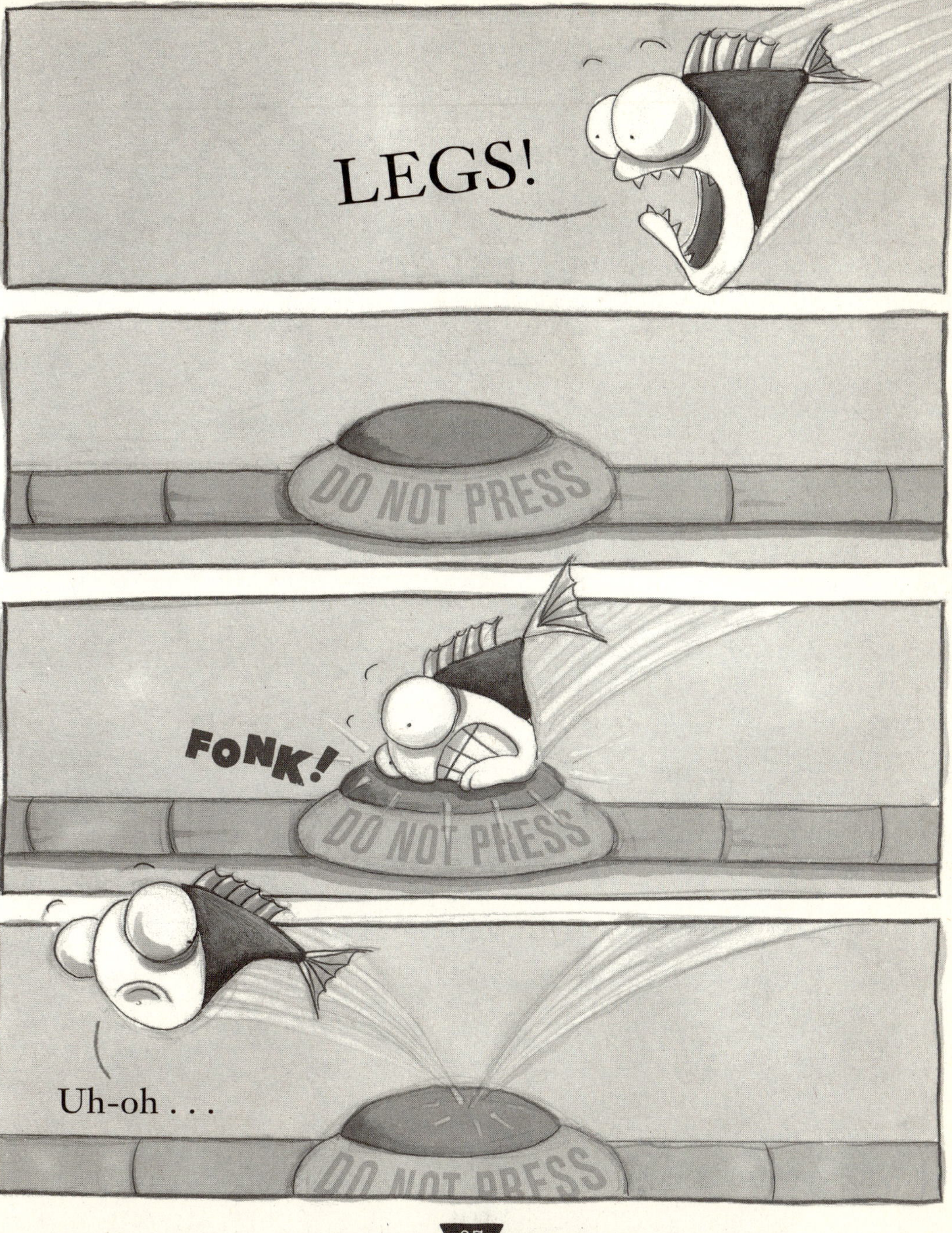
LEGS!
DO NOT PRESS
FONK!
DO NOT PRESS
Uh-oh . . .
DO NOT PRESS

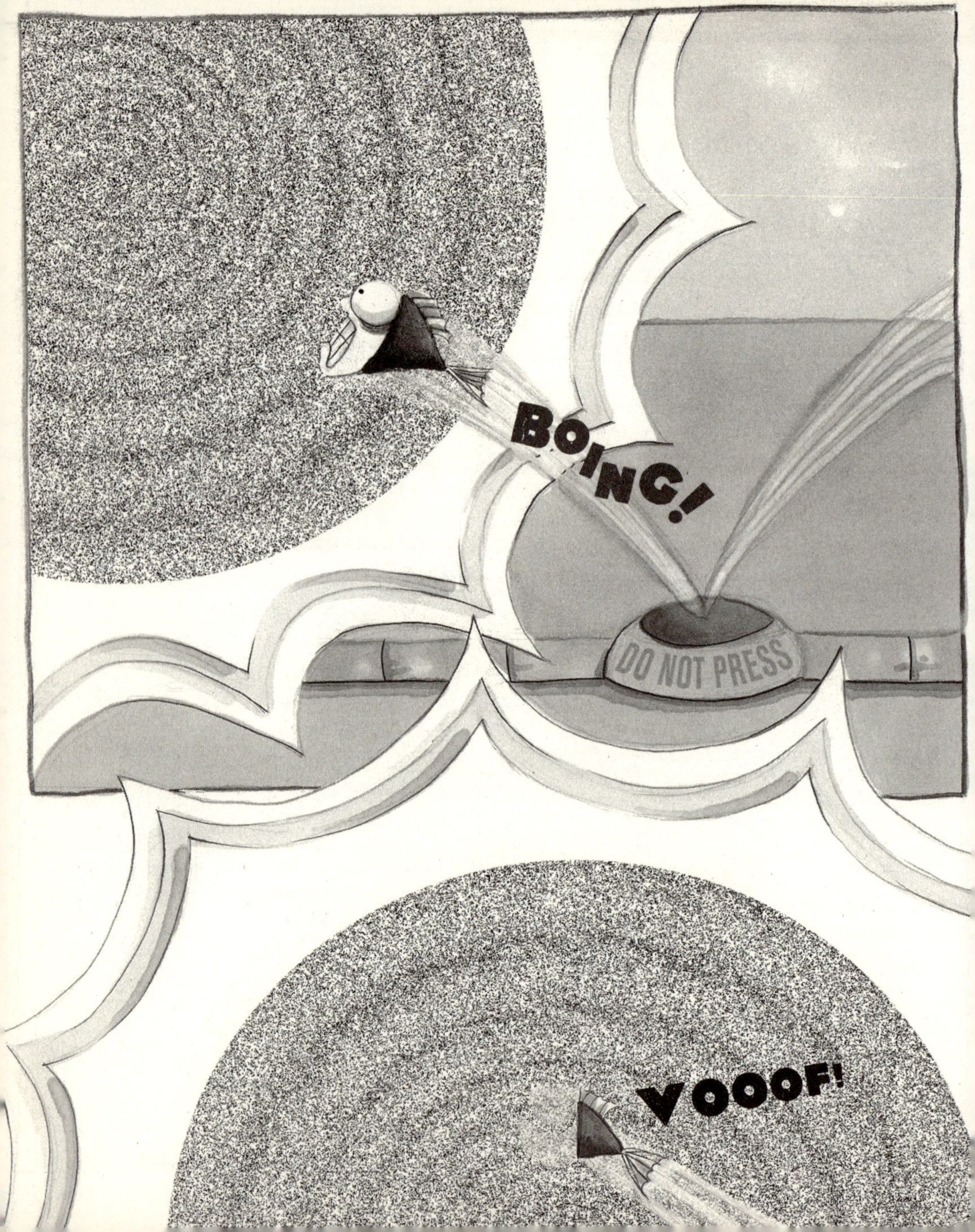
BOING!
DO NOT PRESS
VOOOF!

They jumped into that swirly circle!
Everybody, follow me!

Hey—
what happens if a
VELOCIRAPTOR
follows us into
that thing?

Aw, don't worry about that.

It'll be fine . . .

VOOOF!
SQUARK!
VOOOF!
VOOOF!

VOOOF!

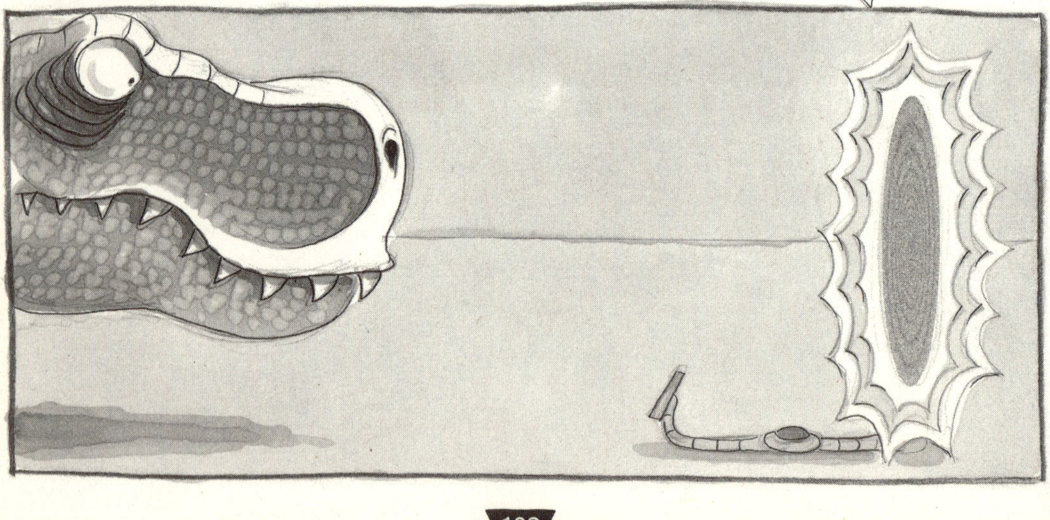

ROOOA-AAARRR-RRR!
STOMP!
CRACK!

FIZZZZZ . . .

• CHAPTER 6 •

ONE WAY TICKET TO WEIRD TOWN

AARRGHHH
BLEEAAARRGGH
WUUURRAAAGGHH
THISSSS IS SOOOO
WEEEIRD!
I HOPE THISSSS
DOESN'T HAVE ANYTHING
TO DOOO WITH THAT
BUTTON I PUSHED!
GGNNNUURGHH

I really hope this is safe.
SQUARK!
Yes. But do you think it's *safe?*
SQUARK!

Do I look strange to you?
In what way?
I don't know.
I just don't feel
like myself . . .

I really wouldn't worry.
CHOCOLATE TROUSERS ARE WONDERFUL!
PASS ME THE FUNNEL!
HOT ELBOWS!
You're not making any sense!
That's a weird thing to say . . .

Do YOU think
this is safe?
You know what?
I feel AWESOME.

Does anyone else feel AWESOME?

What a pleasant journey.
Dude, that was just delightful.

But hey!
Look over there . . .
That looks just like . . .

• CHAPTER 7 •

BACK TO THE . . . YOU KNOW

FOX!
GET OUT
OF THERE!
Stay calm, guys.
Everything will be cool . . .

YOU HAVE BEEN IDENTIFIED
AS AN ENEMY.
PREPARE TO BE
TERMINATED.
Uh-oh . . .

On second thoughts, team . . .
I'd like to ask a favour . . .
POP!
Oh hey!
It *is* you!
LEGS?!

YOU THERE!
FREEZE!!
Oh geez. Hey, man. You should probably watch out . . .

POP!

SMACK!

SPLASH!
FIZZZZ!

Mr Wolf!
You're alive!
Agent Fox!
There's **ALIENS!**
I mean, Marmalade is . . .
I mean, THEY'RE COMING!
Mr Wolf . . .
They're already here.
Oh no.

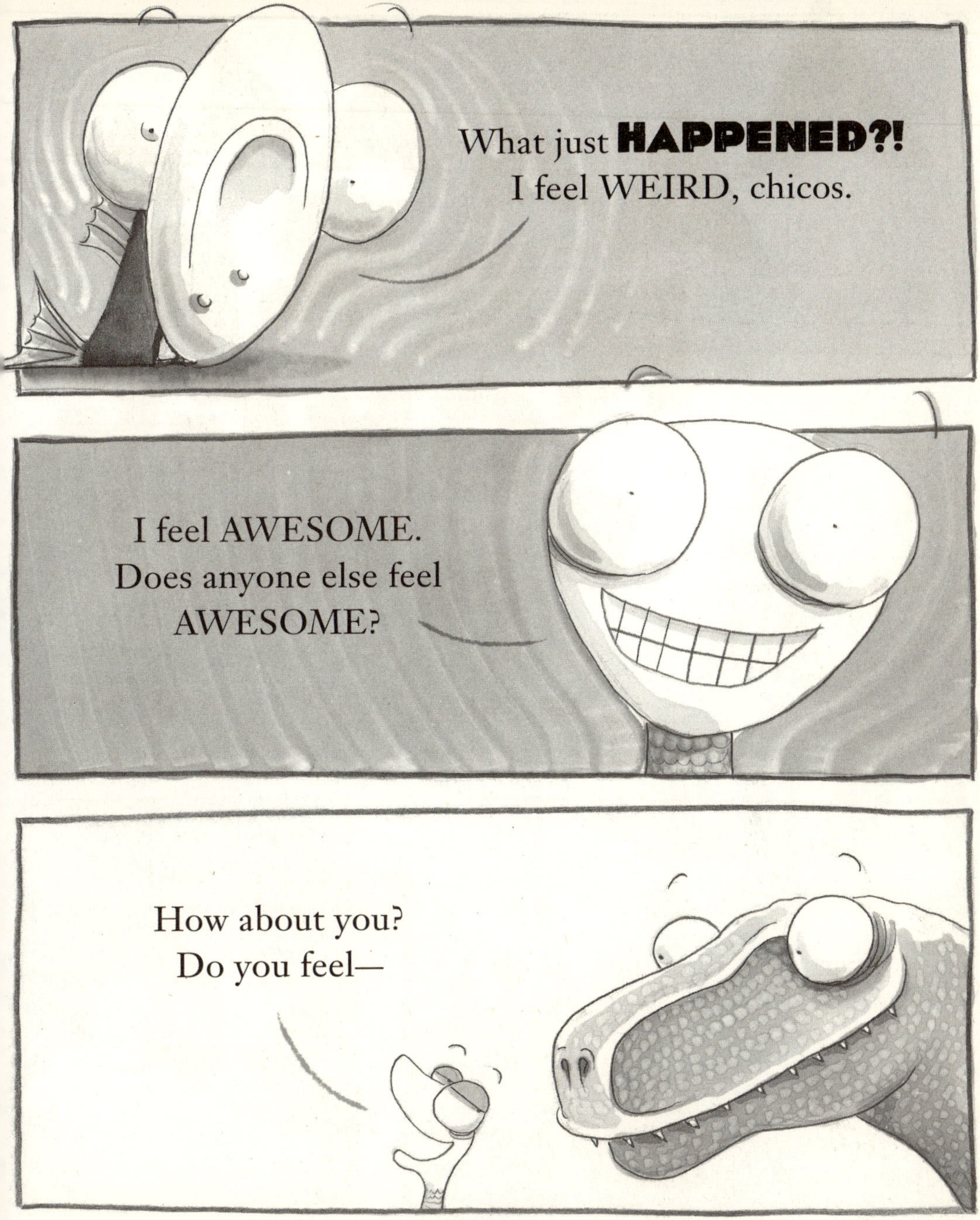
What just **HAPPENED?!**
I feel WEIRD, chicos.
I feel AWESOME.
Does anyone else feel
AWESOME?
How about you?
Do you feel—

AAAAAAARRRRRGGGGHHHH!

Is that what I think it is?!
Agent Fox!
Look out!
It's a dinosaur and—
COUGH! COUGH!

My goodness, what a *kerfuffle!*
I'm terribly sorry, but we've not been formally introduced . . .

My name is
MILTON.
It's a *pleasure*
to meet you . . .

• CHAPTER 8 •

HUH?!

FAAZOOOOM!

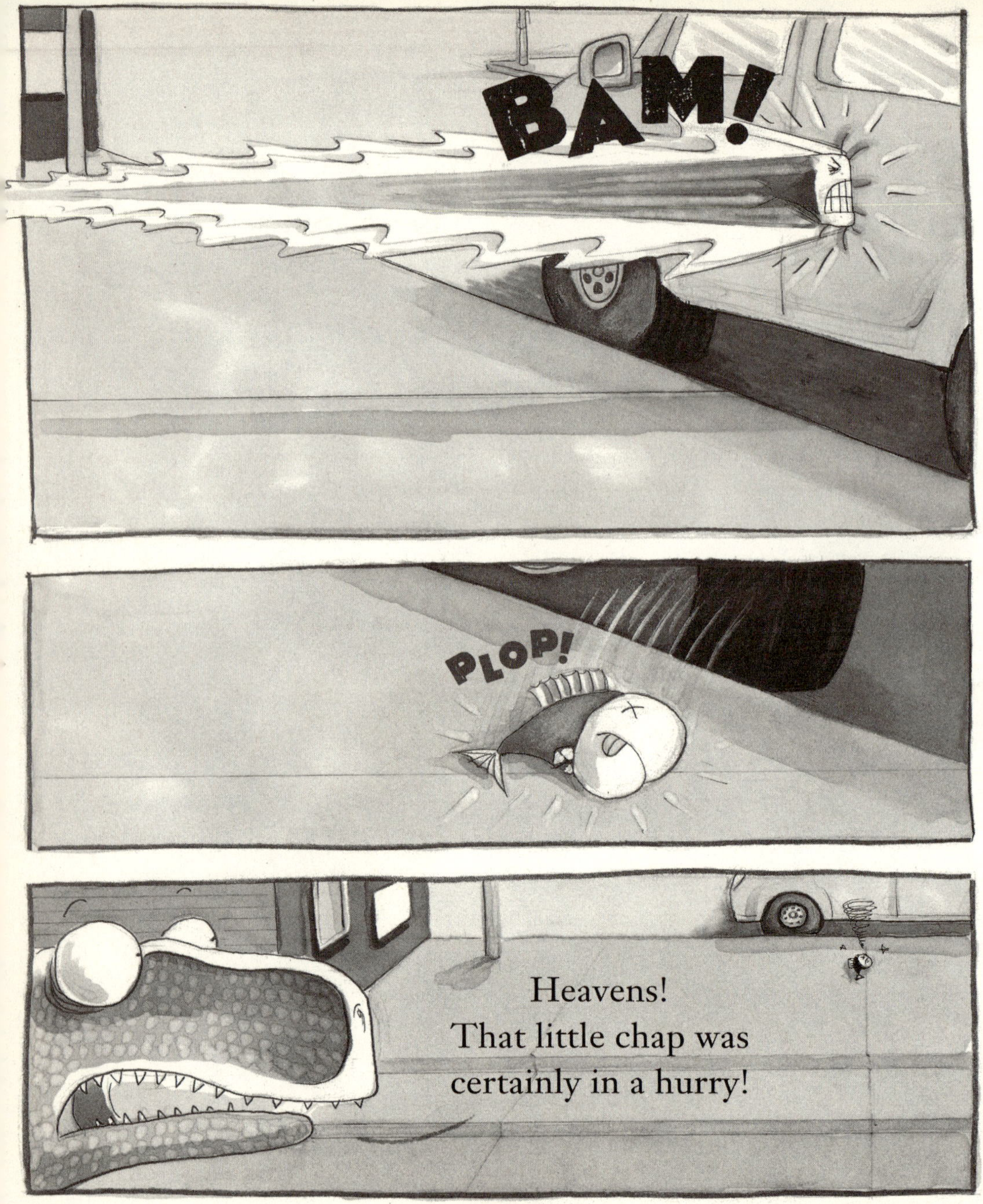
BAM!
PLOP!
Heavens!
That little chap was
certainly in a hurry!

Did you see that?!
He was like a **BULLET!**
I mean, an *actual* bullet.
He was *so* fast . . .
Is he OK?

GASP!
What?!

Seriously . . .
what?

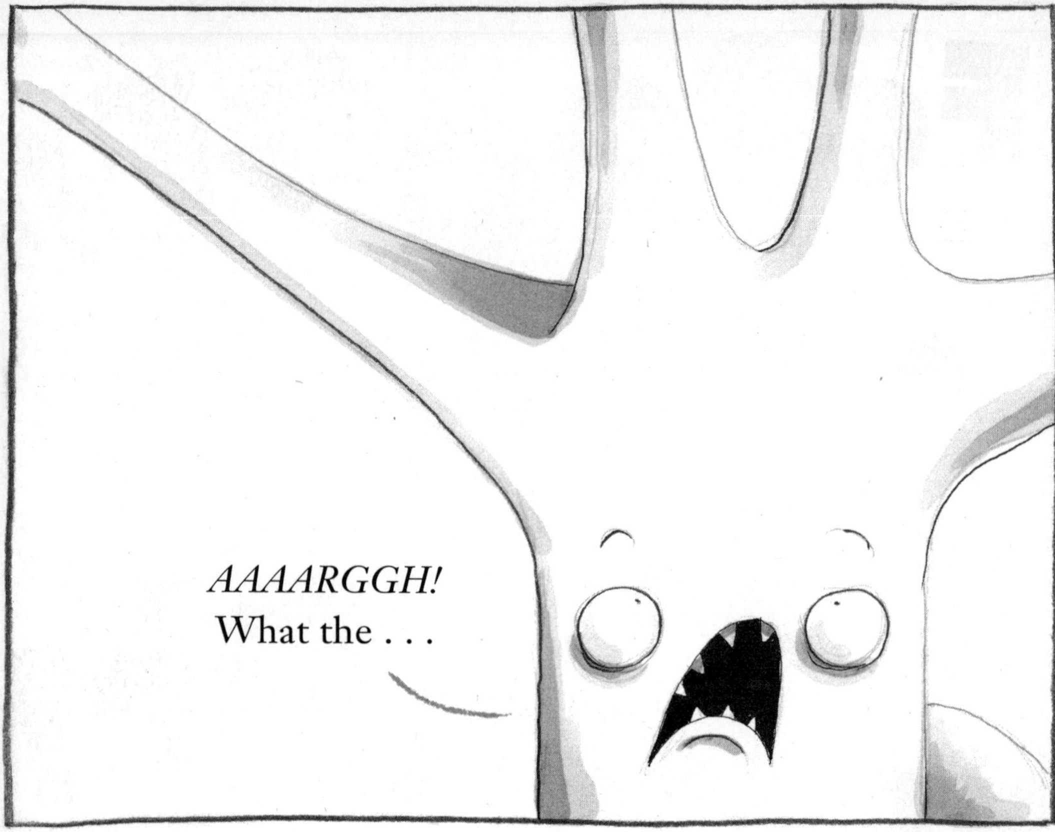
AAAARGGH!
What the . . .

SHAKE!
SHAKE!
SHAKE!
SHAKE!
No no no no no!

FOOOOOF!
Eeeeeeeeeee!
FOOOOOF!
Bleeeauuuurrrgghh!

FOOOOOF!
Bwah-hahaharrrgh!
What's happening to me?!

Mr Shark . . .
You're shape-shifting.
NO
STOPPING
You think
that's cool?
Check this out . . .
SHUDDER!
SHUDDER!

SKM-585

Guys, I think Mr Snake is lifting a car . . .
. . . with his **MIND.**
Mr Wolf?
I feel a little scared.
What's going on here, man?

I'm not sure, buddy.
But if I had to guess . . .
I'd say we've got ourselves some . . .

SUPE
MAIL

RPOWERS!
Well, isn't this
just *marvellous?*
TO BE CONTINUED . . .

SUPER POWERS?! Who saw THAT coming?!

THE BAD GUYS might have got an upgrade,

but does that *guarantee* them a place in

THE INTERNATIONAL LEAGUE OF HEROES?

Nope. But they will be holding **TRYOUTS**...

the BAD GUYS EPISODE 8

SPEEDING TO YOU SOON.

LIKE AN ENHANCED PIRANHA.

The following broadcast was picked up by satellite, while being beamed from Earth into Deep Space . . .

KEEPING UP WITH

KDJFLOER HGCOINW ERUHCGLE IRWFHEKLW JFHXALHW!

Hiiiiiii everyone!
This is soooooooo exciting!
My very own
REALITY TV SHOW!
I could just *die*.
But what's that, you say?
Who IS this disgusting
CUTE and CUDDLY
little creature calling himself
DR RUPERT MARMALADE?
Well, I've only got one thing
to say about that . . .
ZZZZZZZZIP!

SURPRISE!

It’s me!

KDJFLOERHGCO
INWERUHCGLEIR
WFHEKLWJFHXALHW!

Did you miss me?!

Shut **UP!**

Of course you did.

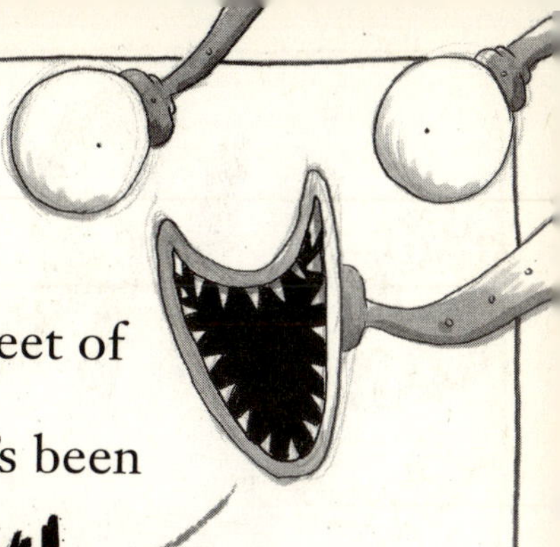

I know you've *all* been wondering what I've been up to since I left our planet with an **ARMY** and a fleet of **WARSHIPS** and all I can say is it's been

ONE BIG PARTY!

You have NO idea . . .

WOOT! WOOT!

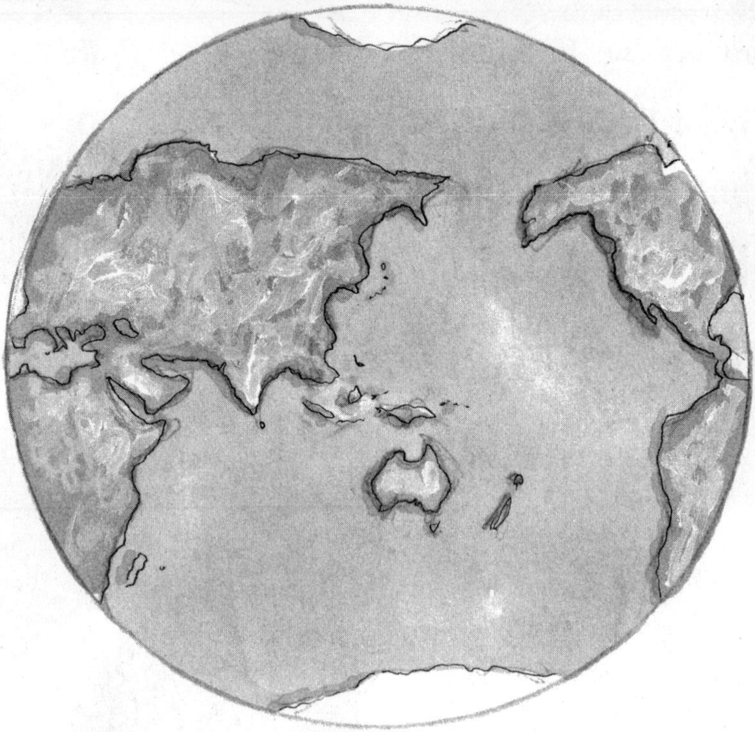

I've been on an

INTERGALACTIC SHOPPING SPREE

and I was like

'OMG, Earth? Yes, please! I'll TAKE IT!'

I just *had* to have it.

BOOM!
Sooooo . . .
THIS is my new planet!
Don't you just LOVE it?!
Let me show you 'round . . .
Help us!
Aaaaaarghh!

I've worked SO hard to make
it my own, you know?

I really wanted to, like, personalise it
and make a real statement with it.

I think it's just so 'me'.

And all the little creatures who lived here are mine now too!

I RULE WITHOUT MERCY.
But at the same time, I'm *super fun* to be around. You know what I mean? I'm SO complicated.

10 THINGS I LOOOOOVE!

1. Having my own planet
2. Showing no pity
3. Chocolate sprinkles
4. Feeling the fear of millions
5. Leading my invading army to victory
6. Annihilating my enemies
7. Cheese sticks
8. Intergalactic domination
9. Watching my enemies lose all hope
10. Skinny jeans

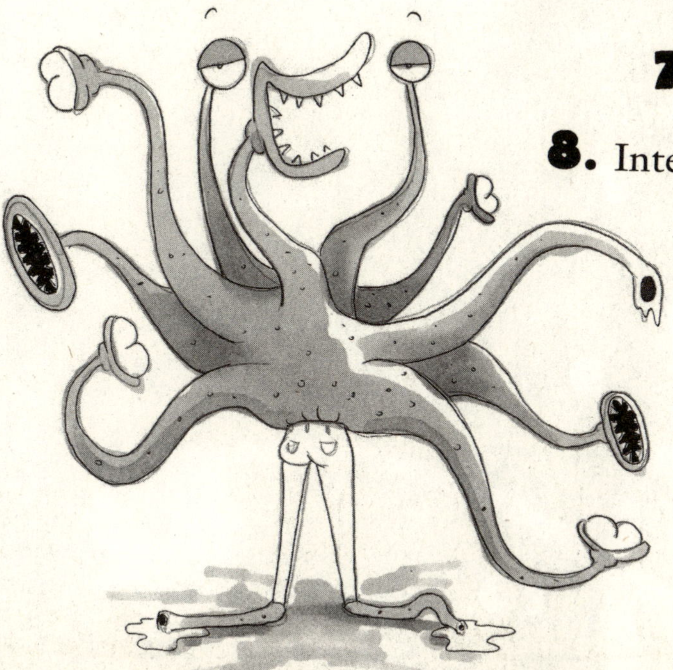

10 THINGS I TOTALLY HATE

1. Being called **CUTE**
2. Being called **CUDDLY**
3. Being called **CUTE AND CUDDLY**
4. Being called anything that implies I'm **CUTE AND CUDDLY** without actually saying it
5. Wolves, Sharks, Snakes, Piranhas and Foxes
   (It's an Earth thing. But don't worry. It's TOTALLY under control.)
6. Body hair (ugh)
7. Running out of cheese sticks
8. Books that end with the words 'To be continued . . .'
9. The happiness of others
10. When a fart goes wrong

My *hopes and dreams?*
Well, I've already accomplished so much, you know? I'm rich. I'm *gorgeous.* I have a planet of my own, with a side order of **ABSOLUTE POWER.**
I've got it all.
So . . . I guess my dream is to wake up tomorrow being just as **PERFECT AS I AM TODAY.**
I think that's something we can ALL relate to.

And to everyone watching back on my BEAUTIFUL HOME PLANET, I'd like to send you this message . . .
For all the INSPIRATION I give you—
You're welcome.